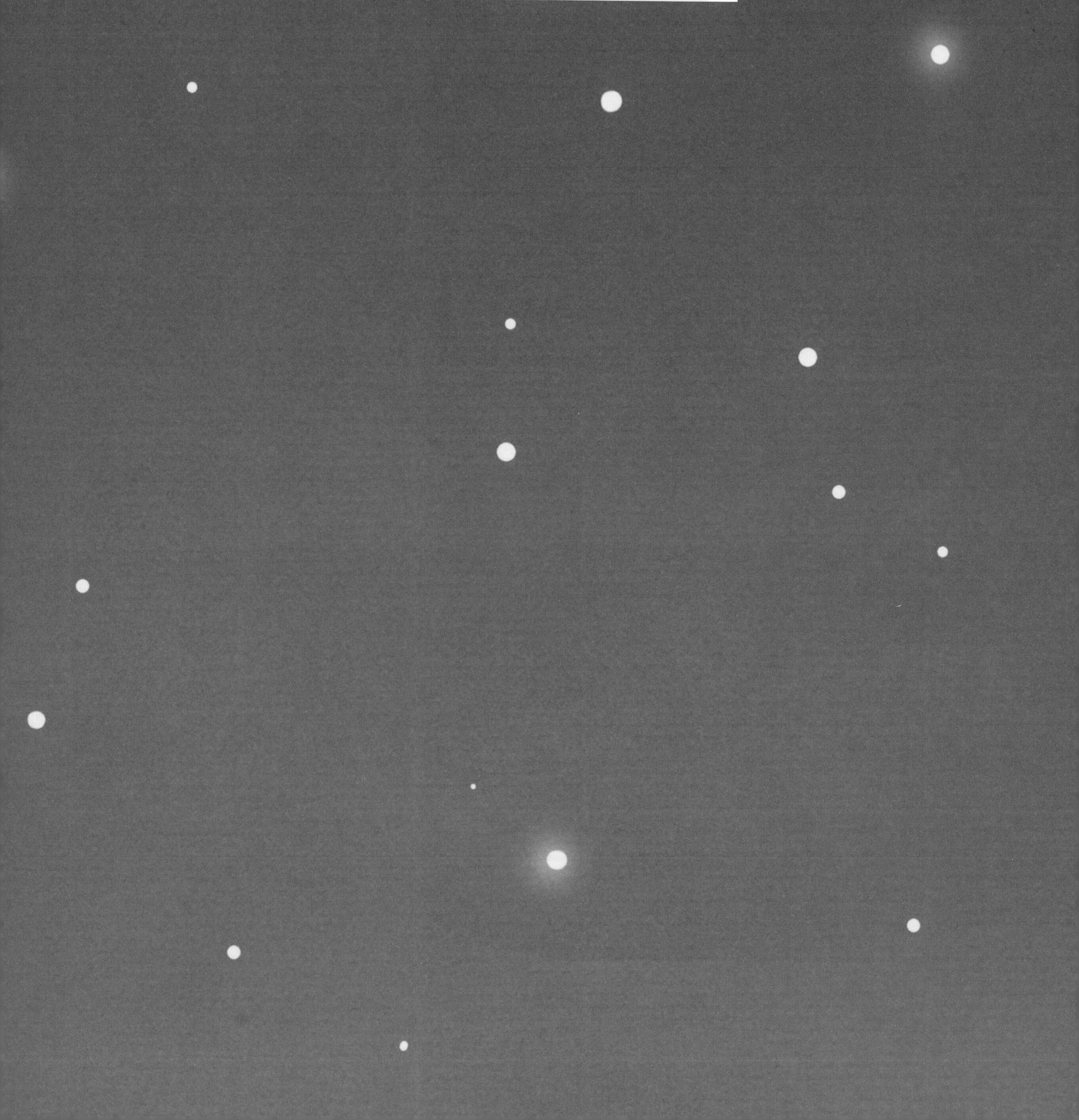

MIX
Paper from
responsible sources
FSC® C118365

First published in Belgium and Holland by Clavis Uitgeverij, Hasselt – Amsterdam, 2015
Copyright © 2015, Clavis Uitgeverij

English translation from the Dutch by Clavis Publishing Inc. New York
Copyright © 2016 for the English language edition: Clavis Publishing Inc. New York

Visit us on the web at www.clavisbooks.com

Mary Has a Baby written by Mieke van Hooft and illustrated by Lonneke Lever
Original title: *Maria krijgt een kindje*
Translated from the Dutch by Clavis Publishing

ISBN 978-1-60537-304-1

This book was printed in June 2016 at Publikum d.o.o., Slavka Rodica 6, Belgrade, Serbia
First Edition
10 9 8 7 6 5 4 3 2 1

Clavis Publishing supports the First Amendment and celebrates the right to read

Mary
Has a Baby

Mieke van Hooft & Lonneke Leever

Clavis

NEW YORK

The moon is shining brightly.
This night is cold and clear.
I hear the hoofs go click-a-clack:
How comes this donkey here?

On its back rides mother Mary.
Her time is drawing near.
Her husband softly comforts her:
"We're almost there, my dear."

Her husband's name is Joseph.
To Bethlehem, they go.
"Donkey, stop! We've made it!"
His voice is grave and low.

"Do you have a room for us?"
They inquire at the inn.
But all the beds are taken,
none for Joseph and his kin.

Wherever will they spend the night?
They're starting to despair.
But there's a stable in the fields,
and they decide to sleep in there.

There is no bed, no table,
just some hay upon the ground.
They huddle 'round the donkey,
sleeping safe and sound.

Mary has her baby.
She rocks him to and fro.
Joseph kisses his sweet forehead.
They love the baby so.

There is no crib, no cradle,
just a manger full of hay.
But a burlap sack becomes a blanket,
and the baby sleeps away.

High up in the mountains
are the shepherds of Bethlehem.
They are startled by an angel,
who brings the news to them:

"Shepherds, listen to my words.
Little sheep, lend an ear.
Baby Jesus has been born,
not so far from here."

The stable gets a visit
from the shepherds and their sheep.
They bring some milk and fire,
for the baby fast asleep.

"Thank you all," kind Joseph says.
"Come in, be welcome here.
Is there someone at the door?
What are those voices that I hear?"

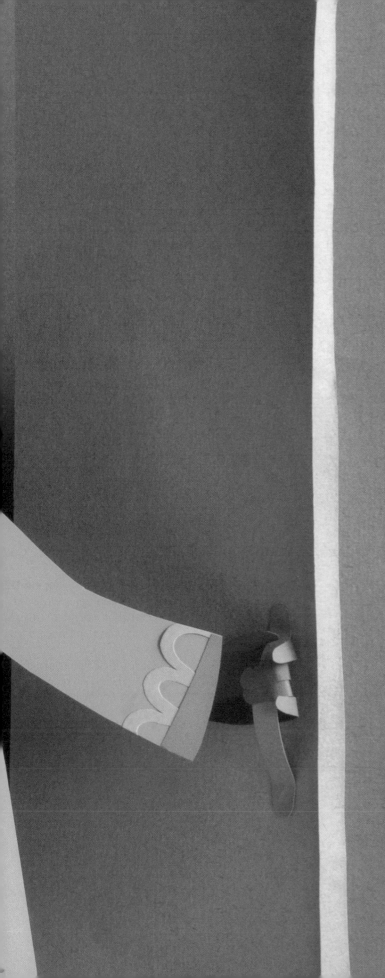

The door then opens once again.
The wind blows raw and cold.
Three wise men enter the stable,
very regal, and very old.

They offer many presents,
and sing a song or two.
Then everybody goes to sleep.
Even the animals are tired, too.

But the good donkey stays awake--
It's such a lovely night.
The child has brought them all
such love, and peace, and light.